W9-CQV-794

# Milk Rock

Jeff Kaufman

Henry Holt and Company New York

To Julie

Special thanks to Laura, Donna, and Martha

Henry Holt and Company, Inc.
*Publishers since 1866*
115 West 18th Street
New York, New York 10011

Henry Holt is a registered
trademark of Henry Holt and Company, Inc.

Copyright © 1994 by Jeff Kaufman
All rights reserved.
Published in Canada by Fitzhenry & Whiteside Ltd.,
195 Allstate Parkway, Markham, Ontario L3R 4T8.

Library of Congress Cataloging-in-Publication Data
Kaufman, Jeff.
Milk Rock / Jeff Kaufman.
Summary: After a year of bad luck, Farmer Foster considers
selling the farm until he discovers a rock that gives milk.
[1. Farm life—Fiction. 2. Rocks—Fiction. 3. Magic—Fiction. 4. Humorous stories.] I. Title.
PZ7.K1644Mi 1994 [E]—dc20 93-41371

ISBN 0-8050-2814-5

First Edition—1994

Printed in the United States of America
on acid-free paper. ∞

1 3 5 7 9 10 8 6 4 2

The illustrations for this book were created with
hand-cut Avery label paper and Chartpak felt markers.

Farmer Foster lived a life of raw hands, sore muscles, long days, and few rewards. Yet season after season, year after year, his hard work made things grow out of the dry, rocky soil.

Then his luck went bad. The rain stopped, and the crops wilted. The chickens ran away. The cow died. Someone stole Roberta, his prize pig. Finally, his truck exploded and burned down half the house.

Farmer Foster was just about to give up, sell the farm, and join his cousin's cleaning supply company in St. Louis, when he remembered his daddy's favorite saying: "Quitters ain't worth spit!"

So, Farmer Foster got out the wheelbarrow and filled it with his most valued possessions: a set of Statue of Liberty place mats, a 1958 Willie Mays baseball card, five jars of homemade strawberry jam, a pair of almost-new work boots, and his mother's old rocking chair. Then he headed into town.

For the rest of the day he wandered from door to door, trying to trade his wares for seed or livestock. Mrs. Spindler at the Laundromat gave him some peanut butter cookies and a free wash-and-dry coupon, but no one else was interested, and no one else would help.

Tired and disheartened, Farmer Foster stopped in a field of weeds, sat back against the wheelbarrow, and fell into a deep, troubled sleep. He dreamed that he was climbing a long, rickety ladder that hung in space like a kite. The ladder started to spin, end over end, faster and faster. He held on for dear life, but his fingers began to slip. Suddenly...

...he was awake! He opened his eyes, staggered to his aching feet, and jumped back with a start. The wheelbarrow, and everything in it, was gone. In its place was a huge, mud-caked rock.

Farmer Foster slowly, carefully stepped closer. He touched the rock and scraped away some dirt. There, carved into its side, were the words "CARE FOR ME AND I WILL CARE FOR YOU."

CARE

"What is this?" he yelled at the sky. "What am I supposed to do?" There was no answer; just the soft rustling of leaves in the nearby trees. "Well, I don't have much choice, do I?" he grumbled as he leaned into the rock and pushed.

It was dark by the time Farmer Foster finally got home. He shoved the rock into the drafty old barn, sat down, rubbed his sore feet, and waited.

Morning came with an unchanged rock, and a stiff and angry Farmer Foster. He muttered a curse and was starting for the door when a sudden tremor shook the farm. Farmer Foster fell to the ground just as a small white drop bubbled up from a crack in the rock's side.

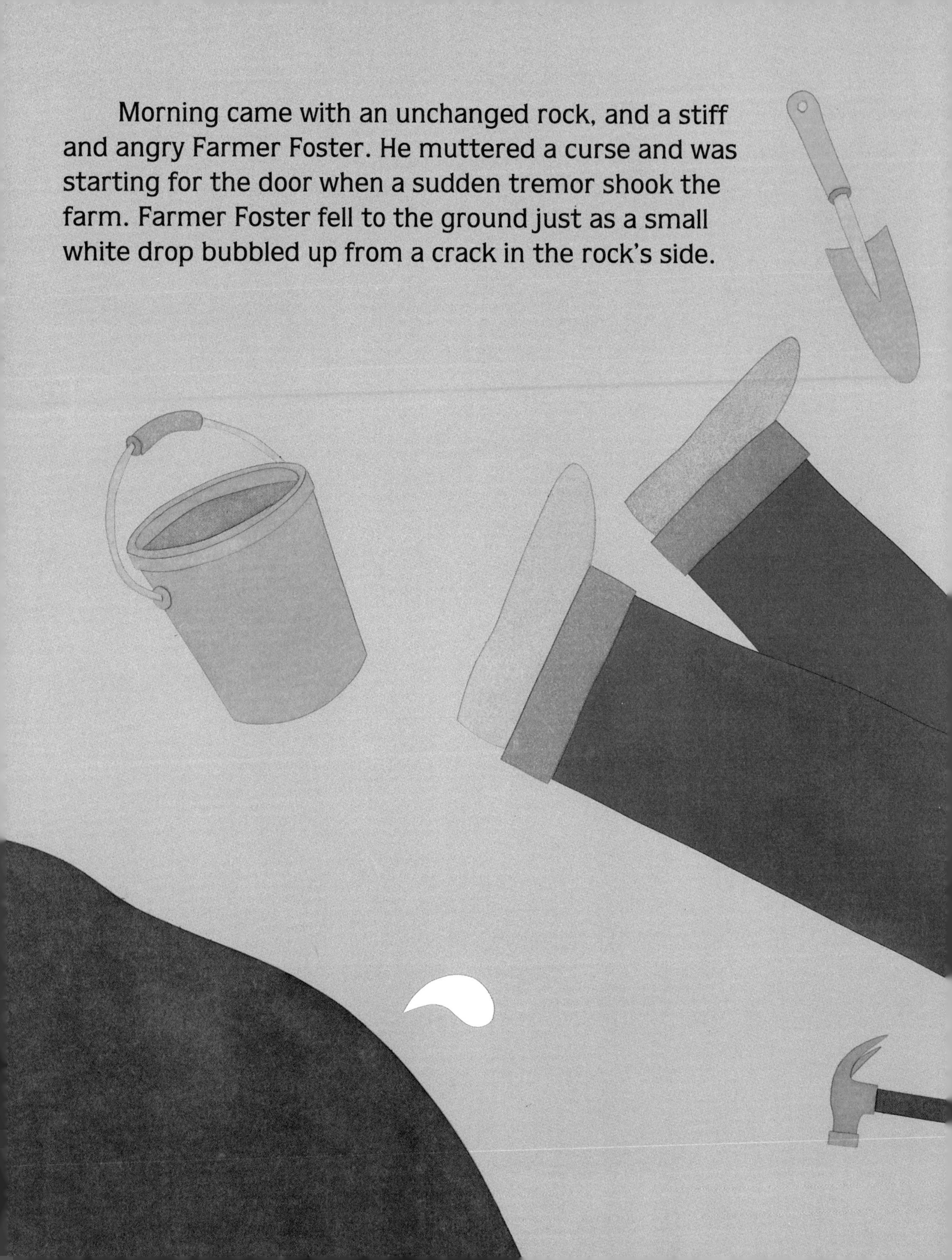

Farmer Foster rushed over and scooped the drop onto his finger. He held it up to the light, sniffed it, and brought it to his lips. His eyes went wide in shock. It was milk! The thickest, creamiest, best-tasting milk he'd ever had. He screamed with joy, hugged the rock, and danced around the barn.

His heart still pounding, Farmer Foster washed and polished the rock, put it on a bed of fresh straw, and gave it the last of his food.

The next day Farmer Foster had a truck pick up forty-seven gallons of milk. When he proudly told the driver where it all came from, the man just laughed. So, Farmer Foster led him into the barn, put a bucket by the rock, and stepped back. A moment later there was another gallon of milk. After the driver got up from his faint, he said that was the most amazing thing he'd ever seen, on or off a farm.

Word spread fast. Neighbors, tourists, and reporters descended on the farm, eager to see the miracle Milk Rock. Farmer Foster and the Milk Rock were on television and in newspapers and magazines. All around the country people tried feeding and milking rocks. No one had any luck, although one man claimed to have coaxed root beer from a lump of coal.

Soon Farmer Foster was able to reseed the land, fix the house, hire some help, and buy new animals. He even started his own line of dairy products: Rock Brand milk, cream, cottage cheese, and three kinds of cheddar. There were plans for guided tours, a restaurant, a water slide, and a Milk Rock motel across the road.

Success felt good. Farmer Foster bought himself a closetful of clothes and a fancy new car and had an Olympic-size pool built where the tomato patch used to be. More and more, the hired hands tended the farm and looked after the Milk Rock while Farmer Foster slept till lunch, then spent the rest of the day in the pool. He got a terrific tan, but gained twenty-two pounds.

Then, late one afternoon, when the first fall breeze chilled the air, Farmer Foster was roused from a nap by a worried farmhand. The rock had stopped giving milk!

Farmer Foster rushed over to the barn and found a pale and shrunken Milk Rock. He called in a veterinarian, but she didn't know where to look, let alone what was wrong. He brought over a geologist, but he just frowned and said, "Rocks don't give milk. Never have, never will." Farmer Foster even flew in a team of psychiatrists from New York. They sat with the rock for three-and-a-half days, but left without saying a word. (They did, however, leave a large bill.)

A week passed, then a month. Farmer Foster bathed the rock. He gave it mineral rubs. He brought it fresh fruit and vegetables and a big bouquets of wildflowers. He set up his stereo in the barn and played his favorite Roy Orbison records. But still no milk. Not a drop.

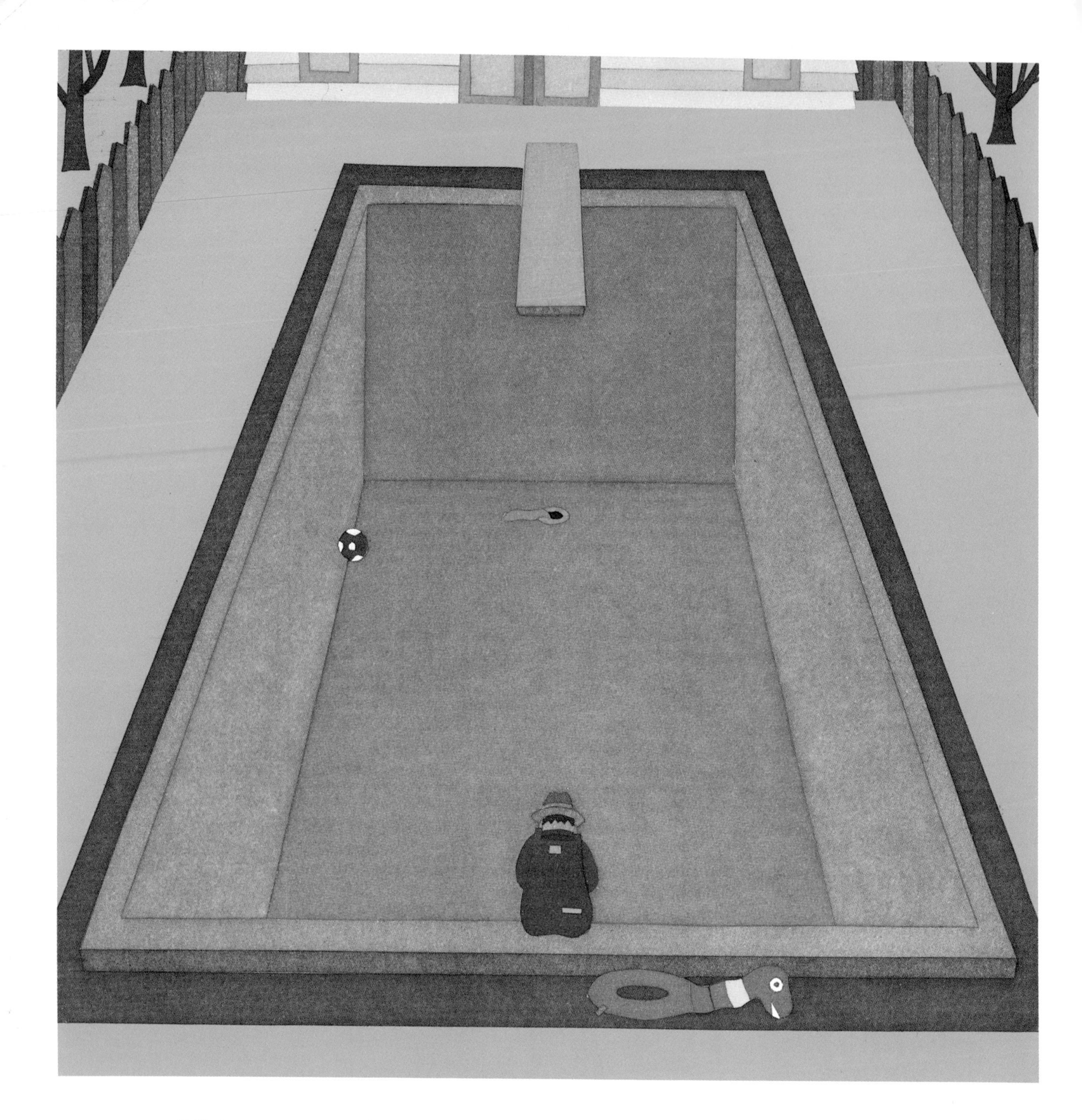

All too soon, the dairy went out of business and the farmhands left, taking the animals for back pay. People started saying that the Milk Rock had been a hoax, and that Farmer Foster should go to jail. The FBI came around to ask questions. The bank foreclosed on the house, drained the pool, and took away the car.

Penniless, Farmer Foster spent the night in the barn next to the rock. He woke with straw stuck in his ear and a businessman standing in the doorway. Flashing a big smile, the man said he wanted to buy the rock, break it up into thousands of pieces, and sell them as Milk Rock paperweights. He promised Farmer Foster a lot of money.

Farmer Foster was tempted, but he shook his head no. The businessman argued till his hairpiece slipped off. Farmer Foster just patted the rock and said, "Sorry, I can't do it." Climbing into his car, the man yelled, "Foster, you're a fool!" and sped away.

At that, the air went still and the ground began to shake. Farmer Foster fell to his knees as the barn swayed above him. He looked at the rock. Something bubbled up out of the crack in its side. Farmer Foster put a drop to his lips. It was fresh-squeezed orange juice! The best he'd ever tasted.